The Quinceañera

Written by **Judith Bauer Stamper**

Illustrated by **Ishan Varma**

TeachingStrategies® · Bethesda, MD

For Teaching Strategies, LLC.
Publisher: Larry Bram
Editorial Director: Hilary Parrish Nelson
VP Curriculum and Assessment: Cate Heroman
Product Manager: Kai-leé Berke
Book Development Team: Sherrie Rudick and Jan Greenberg
Project Manager: Jo A. Wilson

For Q2AMedia
Editorial Director: Bonnie Dobkin
Editor and Curriculum Adviser: Suzanne Barchers
Program Manager: Gayatri Singh
Creative Director: Simmi Sikka
Project Manager: Santosh Vasudevan
Illustrator: Ishan Varma
Designer: Ritu Chopra

Teaching Strategies, LLC.
Bethesda, MD
www.TeachingStrategies.com

ISBN: 978-1-60617-121-9

Library of Congress Cataloging-in-Publication Data
Stamper, Judith Bauer.
 The quinceañera / written by Judith Bauer Stamper ; illustrated by Ishan Varma.
    p. cm.
 Summary: When she is about to turn fifteeen, Rosa's family prepares for her quinceañera by sewing her
a beautiful dress to wear and cooking a magnificent feast to be enjoyed by all. Includes note on how fabric is made.
 ISBN 978-1-60617-121-9
 [1. Quinceañera (Social custom)--Fiction. 2. Family life--Fiction. 3. Hispanic Americans--Fiction.] I. Varma, Ishan, ill. II. Title.
 PZ7.S78612Qu 2010
 [E]--dc22
                                    2009044291

CPSIA tracking label information:
RR Donnelley, Dongguan, China
Date of Production: July 2021
Cohort: Batch 11
Printed and bound in China

14 15 16 17	2021
Printing	Year Printed

Hola! My name is Gabriella. This is my big sister, Rosa. She will be fifteen soon. For her birthday, Rosa will have a quinceañera. It is a special celebration for a fifteen-year-old girl.

This is my family: Rosa, Mama, Abuela, Papa, and my brother, Eduardo.

Everyone will help Rosa celebrate her quinceañera.

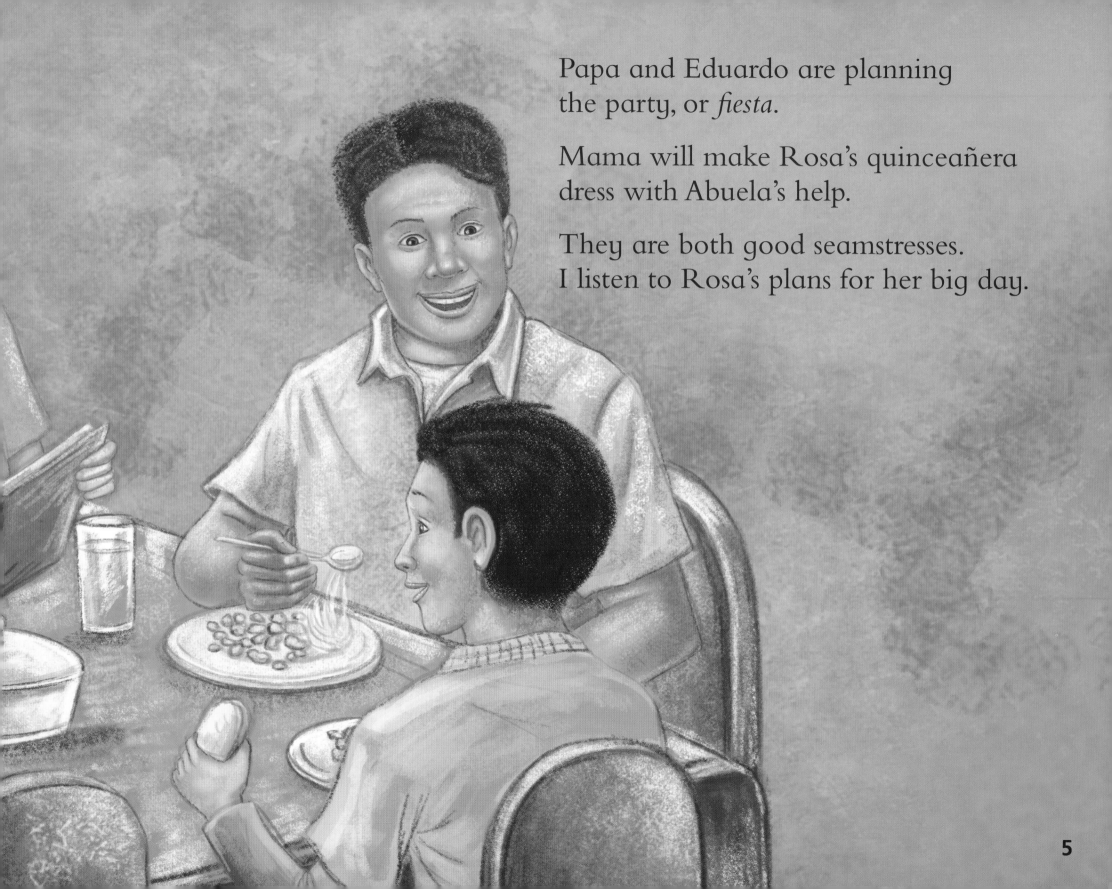

Papa and Eduardo are planning
the party, or *fiesta*.

Mama will make Rosa's quinceañera
dress with Abuela's help.

They are both good seamstresses.
I listen to Rosa's plans for her big day.

Mama and Rosa take me with them to a big fabric store. It has rows and rows of cloth.

We love to look at the pictures from Rosa's quinceañera. My family is very happy and proud.

In ten years, I will be fifteen. And I will have a beautiful quinceañera dress, too. I can't wait!

How Is Cloth Made?

Cloth is made from natural or man-made fibers.
Natural fibers come from plants or animals.

Cotton is made from the cotton plant.
Linen is made from the flax plant.
Wool comes from sheep.
Silk is made by silkworms.

Some fibers are made by machines in factories.
Examples are rayon, nylon, and polyester.

Cloth is manufactured by weaving yarns together on a loom.

A hand loom is operated by a person.
A factory loom is operated by machines and can make
miles of fabric in a day.

Knit fabric is made by looping yarn together
with two long, pointed needles or on a machine.
Crochet fabric is made by looping yarn together with a hooked needle.